OH NO!
There's a monster in your book!

Let's try to get him out.

shake the book
and turn the page . . .

Nice try – that knocked him over, but he's
STILL IN YOUR BOOK!

Tickle
his feet and turn the page . . .

That didn't work – he's just laughing and he's
STILL IN YOUR BOOK!

Try blowing him away.

BLOOW

really hard and turn the page . . .

That's better – now he's far away, but he's
STILL IN YOUR BOOK!

TILT the book to the left . . .

Now he's over here, but he's . . .

STILL IN YOUR BOOK!

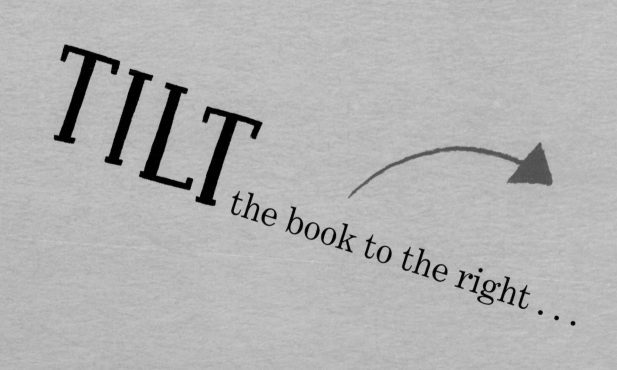

TILT the book to the right . . .

He's hanging on!

What a naughty little monster!

Give the book a good

wiggle...

OK, now he's back over there.
But there's **STILL** a monster in your book!

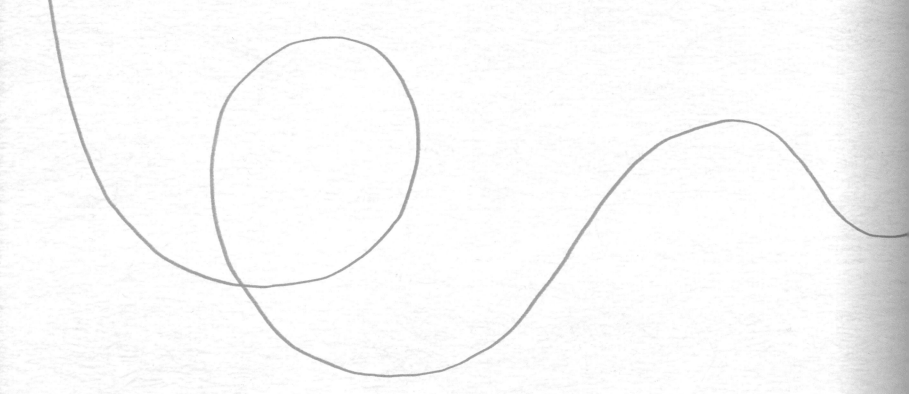

Try **spinning** the book round and round . . .

Look! He's dizzy!

Quick, make a

LOUD

noise . . .

It's working! He's running away!

Make that noise again, but . . .

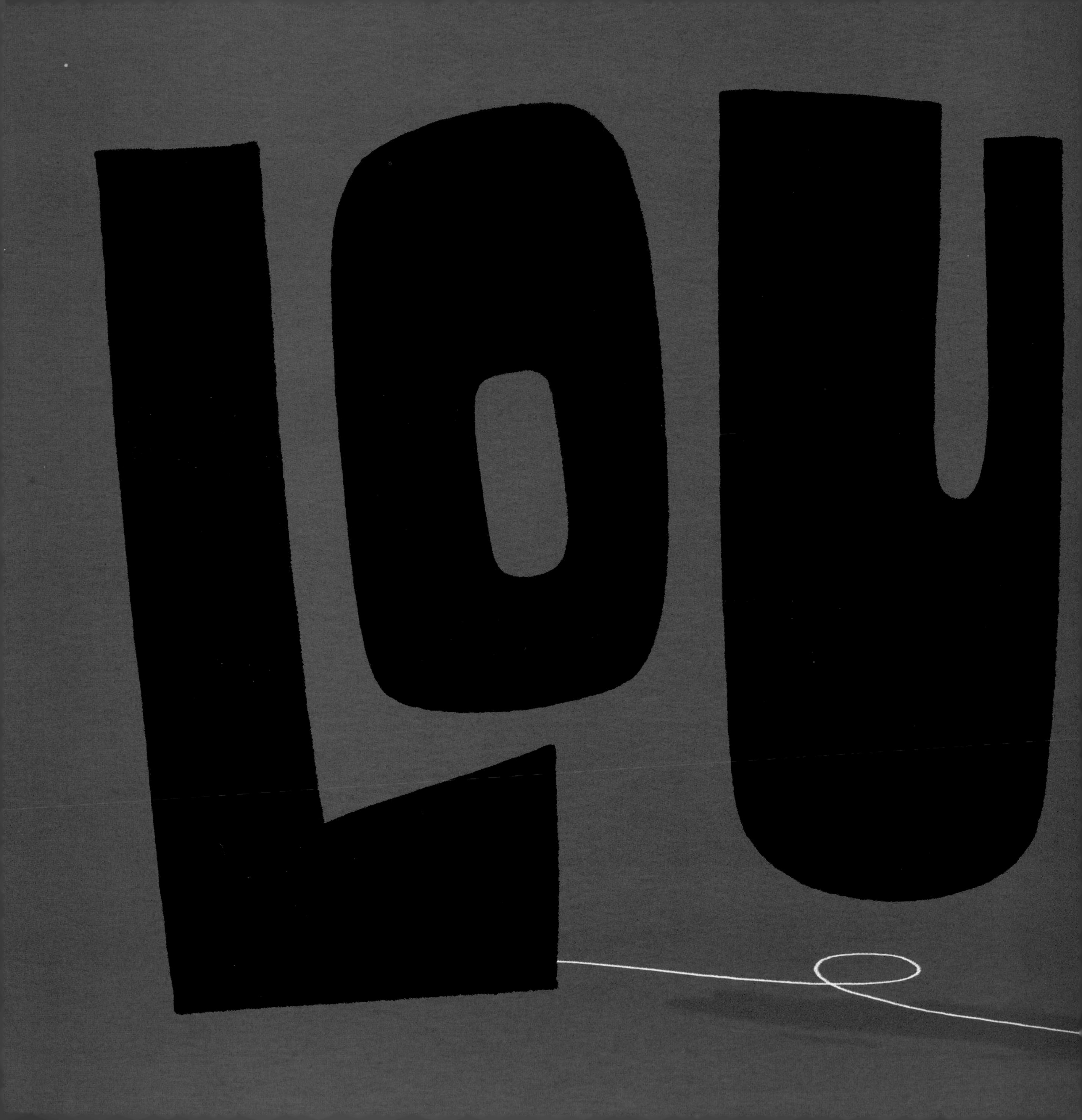
LOU

HE'S GONE!

There **ISN'T** a monster in your book any more . . .

Now he's in your room!

Quickly, call him back . . .
Monster, come back!

Look! Here he is!
He's coming back.

Keep calling him . . .

Monster!

Come here, little monster!

PHEW!

He's back in your book.

You don't want a monster loose in your room!
This book is probably the best place to keep him.

Monster, you can stay here in this book!

Stroke Monster's head and say goodnight . . .

Goodnight, Monster.

SHHH!
Look! He's fast asleep.

Gently close the book so he doesn't wake up.